Detective Dog®
Goes on Vacation

Detective Dog®
Goes on Vacation

Written by Leslie McGuire
Illustrated by Mitchell Rose

Contents

Special Words

Special words help make this story fun.
Your child may need help reading them.

closet

room

space

vacation

voice

1 I Need a Rest!

This is Detective Dog. He looks for lost pets. He helps get them back. He looks for lots of lost stuff—not just pets. It's a very difficult job, but he has to do it because no one does it as well as he can. He is the best detective there is. He is very good at his job!

But Detective Dog needs a vacation now and then.

"What can I do?" he says. "I am the best detective there is, but I cannot be a good detective with no rest at all! I just have to trust that no pets or other big stuff gets lost until I get back."

Detective Dog gets on the bus at six o'clock. He does not say where he is going. He does not want Pig, Rabbit, Cat, and Duck to come after him. They will make him look for all of the stuff they just lost.

Detective Dog gets to Duck Pond Inn at ten o'clock and checks in.

"Welcome," says the bellhop. "Let me take your bags."

"Thank you. This is the best vacation spot," he says as they go up to his room. "I can catch fish here and play chess and checkers. I can sit here for days and get a lot of rest!"

"This is a good room, too," says Detective Dog. "I can see the pond where I will swim and catch fish."

"You can see the moon, too," says the bellhop, "and have a snack in your room if you like."

"I like that," says Detective Dog.

Detective Dog unpacks his bag
and puts all of his things in the
closet. He wants to rest, so he asks
for a snack in bed. He picks a
chicken sandwich and a pumpkin
muffin. But when he goes to put
on his slippers, they are not there!

"How can this be? I put all of my stuff in the closet. So where are my slippers?" he asks himself. "I put them right here as soon as I checked in! This is very odd. I am the best detective there is, and I cannot find my slippers!"

Detective Dog looks in his bag. "Maybe I forgot to take them out."

He looks under the bed. "Maybe I hid them."

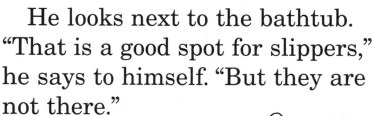

He looks next to the bathtub. "That is a good spot for slippers," he says to himself. "But they are not there."

He looks on top of the dresser.
"Not up here."

He looks in back of the TV.
"No slippers."

"I will just have to get new slippers," says Detective Dog.

That's when he begins to look for his brush. It's not there!

"This is very, very odd," says Detective Dog. "I do not like this at all!"

"Did someone come in my room and take my stuff?" he asks himself. "No, that could not be right. I have been here all of this time! Maybe I just forgot to bring them."

But then he thinks about that.

"This is a big problem," he says to himself. "Things are missing, and I did not take them. That means there must be people I cannot see in my room taking my stuff. That is bad!"

Then Detective Dog stops to think. "The problem is that people you cannot see are ghosts."

2 No Such Thing as a Ghost

Detective Dog is thinking about Jack's kitten. That was one of his big jobs. People said the kitten was a ghost. But Jack's kitten was not a ghost. He was just a little jumping cat with a blanket on top of him.

"What is the matter with me?"
says Detective Dog. "THERE
ARE NO GHOSTS!"

Detective Dog has to sit down.
"What can it be?" he mutters.
"Who can it be?"

23

"I need to think," says Detective Dog. He gets out his pad.

1. My SLIPPERS ARE GONE.
2. My BRUSH IS MISSING.
3. THERE ARE NO GHOSTS!
4. CHECK OUT THE PEOPLE AT THIS INN.

Detective Dog goes down to see
what he can do. He is very grumpy.
"This is not resting!" he mutters.
He looks over at the bellhop. The
bellhop does not have on slippers.

He sees a man with a fishing hat and sunglasses who has on slippers—but they are not like his slippers.

Then he sees his slippers! They are right next to a big plant. He quickly runs to get them.

But when he gets to the plant,
the slippers are not there!
   That's when he sees his pal Pig.
   "What are YOU doing here?"
asks Detective Dog.
   "I...um...needed a rest, too!"
says Pig.

"You are here on MY vacation," says Detective Dog. "Why? Did you come here to snatch my slippers? What did you do with them?"

Pig gets very upset. "That is not a good thing to say, and I did not take your slippers! I have on MY slippers!"

Detective Dog looks this way and that. "My slippers were just here! If you did not take them, then who did?"

"I do not know," says Pig. "But I will help you look for them."

"You can help me look for my brush," mutters Detective Dog. "That's missing, too!"

They go to check out all of the spots where Detective Dog's slippers could be hidden.

"Detective Dog," says Pig, as they go down to the pond, "you are the best detective ever, and I am just a pig. How come you need help to look for your slippers?"

"Good detectives need help now and then," says Detective Dog.

Then Detective Dog sees the dock! "Oh my!"

3 Why Are You Here?

Detective Dog looks at the dock. He blinks. "What?!"

There, sitting on the dock, is his pal Cat. His pal Duck is swimming in the pond. His pal Rabbit is there, too.

"Look, I am fishing!" yells Rabbit. "I do not like fish, but I like fishing a lot!"

"Why are you all here?" asks Detective Dog. "I am on vacation. I do not want to look for your lost stuff."

"You do not have to! We are on vacation, too!" says Cat. "We just wanted to be with you!"

"That's silly," says Detective Dog.

"It is not," says Rabbit.

"I happen to be a duck," says Duck, "so I can come to Duck Pond Inn if I want to!"

"Did you take my slippers?" yells Detective Dog. "I bet you have my brush, too!"

"No, we did not!" they all yell back at him. "But we will help you get them back!"

"Where do you want us to look?" asks Pig.

"All over," says Detective Dog. "But I did see my slippers back at the inn. They were right next to a big plant!"

"Let's go look!" say Pig, Duck, Cat, and Rabbit.

They all rush into the inn and begin to pick up all of the things they see. They look here! They look there! They look over and under people. They crash into potted plants. They tip things over! They make a big mess.

But they do not see Detective Dog's slippers and brush.

"Stop that!" people yell.

"What are you doing?" yells the bellhop. He looks upset.

That's when Detective Dog looks up and sees his slippers. They are up on the landing by a ladder.

"How did they get up there?" he asks. "Can slippers fly?"

"I will just fly up and grab them," says the bellhop.

But as the bellhop flaps up, the slippers hop up the ladder and hop right out of the inn. He gasps! The slippers land on a big bush.

"Get the slippers!" they all yell, and they all rush out after them.

"I need a rest," says Detective Dog. "I need to sit down. I need to think!"

He takes out his pad.

"Why is this happening to me?"
asks Detective Dog.

All of his pals come back huffing and puffing.

"We could not catch your slippers," they say. "But we did see where they went. They went to the shed. Then they flopped on the grass. Just now, they ran over to the pond."

"But one slipper has your brush," says Pig.

"Now I know where my brush went," says Detective Dog. "We need to catch the slippers now! But how?"

"We need a net!" says Rabbit.

"I will get one," says the bellhop.

Slippers from Planet X?

When the bellhop gets back with the net, the slippers are not there.

"Where did they go?" he asks.

"We do not know," says Rabbit. "I bet Detective Dog's slippers are from outer space!"

"I need to think about this," says Detective Dog. "Why do I keep thinking about ghosts? Maybe it's because I know slippers cannot fly. But there are no ghosts! I bet you are right. It could be outer space beings! That's all that's left!"

"I need my pad," says
Detective Dog.

He checks his left pocket and
says, "I need to look at my list!"

Then he looks in his right pocket.
"Where did I put that silly pad?"

He checks all of his pockets. "I just had it!"

But Detective Dog cannot find his pad at all.

"DRAT!" he yells. "Now my pad is missing, too! I cannot stand it when stuff like this happens! This is not a very good vacation!"

Detective Dog gets up and runs
back to the inn as fast as he can
go! He does not stop to chat. He
does not stop for snacks. He goes
up to his room.

"What I need is a plan!" he says to himself.

"I know!" he says. "I bet I do not need my pad. All I need to do is to think of all of the things that have happened."

Detective Dog sits on his bed and thinks of all of the things he put down on his pad.

"My slippers are not here," he says to himself. "My brush is not here. My pad is missing."

He thinks and thinks.

"My pals did not take them," he says. "But now my slippers can hop."

He thinks and thinks.

"I cannot see who is taking my stuff," he mutters. "But there are no ghosts! Could it be people from outer space?"

He thinks and thinks.

"But there are no people from outer space," he says to himself. "Maybe I am nuts!"

Detective Dog says, "I think I will take a quick nap. After all, I need rest, and I have not gotten a bit of rest yet!"

Detective Dog gets into bed, but he cannot stop thinking. That is when he looks up and sees his pad fly past and zip into the closet.

5 Bad Manners

Detective Dog is upset!
   "Who are you?" he whispers.
   A voice says, "We do not want
to tell!"

"Do I know you?" asks
Detective Dog.

"No," the voice says, "but we
know you!"

"Now I know I am nuts!" says
Detective Dog to himself.

"What do you want?" asks Detective Dog. He does not think he wants to know this. He feels a bit wobbly.

"We want to be your pal," says the voice. "We do not have pals."

"How come?" asks Detective Dog. "We think we do not have pals because we are little," it says.

"What are you?" asks Detective Dog. "Are you from outer space?"

"OUTER SPACE!" yells the voice. "How could you think such a silly thing?"

"Well it's very silly to take slippers and a brush, too!" snaps Detective Dog.

"We know, but we could not help it," says the voice. "We were very bad to do that."

"Bad manners," snaps Detective Dog.

While he says that, he is planning to jump up and grab whatever it is that he cannot see.

Just then, he sees two green blobs jumping up and down by the closet.

"You better tell me who you are," snaps Detective Dog, "because I do not like this."

"Do we have to?"

"Yes!" says Detective Dog.

"OK, OK, OK!"

"I am Fred Frog!" whispers the voice. "This is Frank Frog."

That's when Detective Dog sees two green blobs sitting right next to him.

"Frogs?" he says. "You must be kidding!"

"How can frogs make my slippers run all over?" asks Detective Dog.

"We hid in them," says Fred Frog. "You could see the slippers, but you could not see us in them."

Just then, Rabbit, Pig, Cat, and Duck run into his room.

"Your slippers and your brush are right out there," says Cat.

"Look!" says Duck. "Frogs!"

"I like frogs a lot," says Pig.

"Frogs can hop better than rabbits," says Rabbit. "Will you tell me your hopping tricks?"

The frogs are hidden in back of Detective Dog. It is all too much for them.

"Are you mad at us?" the frogs ask.

"No, we like you," says Pig.

"I did not think that frogs liked to snatch slippers," says Detective Dog.

"Maybe they need slippers for their little frog feet," says Pig.

"My slippers are too big for frogs," says Detective Dog.

"Do you want to have a vacation with us?" asks Rabbit.

"You bet!" say the frogs with a grin.

"I do not think that is all you want," says Detective Dog.

"Well...no," say Fred and Frank. "We want a job! We want to be detectives like you!"

"Do I need helpers?" asks Detective Dog. "Yes, I do! You will be a very big help to me because you are so little. People cannot see you!"

And that is how Detective Dog got Fred and Frank to be his helpers, and how Fred and Frank got Detective Dog for a pal!